For my dad, who bought us comic books every Sunday. (Some things you never forget!)—NK

For Dexter, Nicko & Elias—AB

GROSSET & DUNLAP
Penguin Young Readers Group
An Imprint of Penguin Random House LLC

Text copyright © 2016 by Nancy Krulik. Illustrations copyright © 2016 by Aaron Blecha. All rights reserved. Published by Grosset & Dunlap, an imprint of Penguin Random House LLC, 345 Hudson Street, New York, New York 10014. GROSSET & DUNLAP is a trademark of Penguin Random House LLC. Printed in the USA.

Library of Congress Cataloging-in-Publication Data is available.

ISBN 978-0-448-48285-9   10 9 8 7 6 5 4 3 2 1

George Brown, CLASS CLOWN

It's a Bird, It's a Plane, It's Toiletman!

by Nancy Krulik

illustrated by Aaron Blecha

Grosset & Dunlap

An Imprint of Penguin Random House

Chapter 1

"It's so cold out here my **boogers** are freezing," George Brown told his friend Alex as the boys trudged through the snow on their way to their friend Chris's house.

"This wind is making my eyes tear," Alex said. "It's lucky the salt in tears keeps them from freezing. Can you imagine having **icy eyeballs**?"

"The only good thing about it being so cold," George said, "is that none of the grown-ups are going to want to go outside and shovel their own walks, which means **more money** for us."

George reached up and pushed Chris's doorbell. A minute later Chris came to the door—*in his pajamas*!

"You can't shovel in those," Alex told him. "Put on your **snow pants**. We've got to get to work before some other kids start a shoveling business."

Chris shook his head. "I can't shovel today," he told the boys.

"What are you talking about?" George said. "We planned it all out last night when they announced school was going to be closed."

"I know," Chris admitted. "But I'm working on my new **Toiletman** comic book. And I'm really on a roll. I can't stop now."

George frowned. He knew Chris loved making his **comic books**. *But they were talking money here!* "Can't you draw later?" he asked.

"No. I have to get at least five pages drawn today to stay on **my schedule**," Chris explained.

Alex and George looked at each other. What was Chris talking about?

"What schedule?" Alex asked him.

"Rodney said if I can draw a twenty-two-page Toiletman comic book, he would print it for me and sell it as a **limited edition**," Chris explained. "He's doing a special local-artists'-week promotion at his store. If I want to be part of it, I have to get this done really fast!"

"Wow," George said. That was **impressive**. Rodney was the owner of the Made for Mutants Comic Book Shop. If Rodney thought Chris's Toiletman comic was good enough to sell, it had to be really terrific.

"I'm sorry, guys," Chris apologized. "But I can't shovel snow with you today."

"It's okay," Alex said. "Come on,
George."

George nodded. "**Good luck** with the
comic," he told Chris. "We'll see you in
school tomorrow." He looked out at the
mounds of snow and the gray clouds
overhead. "If there is school," he added.
"You never know. It might snow again
today!"

"Think of it this way," Alex said a little while later as he and George shoveled the snow that had piled up outside George's mom's **craft shop**, Knit Wits. "We only have to split the money two ways, which means more money for each of us."

"True." George added a **big pile** of snow to the mound he and Alex were building off to the side of the store.

"What are you going to do with your cash?" Alex asked him.

George didn't answer. He couldn't. He was afraid to open his mouth. **Something awful** might slip out if he did.

Bing-bong. Ping-pong.

The *something awful* was already bouncing around inside his belly.

There were bubbles in there. Hundreds of them. And they weren't ordinary run-of-the-mill stomach bubbles, either. They were magical **super-burp bubbles**. And there would be trouble if those bubbles broke loose. There was *always* trouble when the magical super burp came around.

George's bubble trouble had started right after his family moved to Beaver Brook. George's dad was in the army, and his family moved around a lot, which meant George had been the **new kid** in school lots of times. So he understood that first days could be rotten. But this first day was the **rottenest**.

In his old school, George was the class clown. But George had promised himself that things were going to be different this time. No more pranks. No more making funny faces behind teachers' backs. Unfortunately, George didn't have to be a **math whiz** to figure out how many friends a new, unfunny kid makes on his first day of school. Zero. None. Nada.

That night, George's parents took him out to Ernie's Ice Cream Emporium just to cheer him up. While they were sitting outside and George was finishing his root beer float, a **shooting star** flashed across the sky. So George made a wish.

I want to make kids laugh—but not get into trouble.

Unfortunately, the star was gone before George could **finish the wish**. So only half came true—the first half.

A minute later, George had a funny feeling in his belly. It was like there were hundreds of *tiny bubbles* bouncing around in there. The bubbles ping-ponged their way into his chest, and bing-bonged their way up into his throat. And then . . .

George let out a big burp. A huge burp. A SUPER burp!

The super burp was loud, and it was *magic*.

Suddenly George **lost control** of his

arms and legs. It was like they had minds of their own. His hands grabbed straws and stuck them **up his nose** like a walrus. His feet jumped up on the table and started dancing the **hokey pokey**.

9

Everyone at Ernie's Ice Cream Emporium started **laughing**—except George's parents, who were covered in the ice cream he'd kicked over while he was dancing.

After that night, the burp came back over and over again. And every time it did, it made **a mess of things**. That was why George couldn't let that burp burst out of him now—*not right in front of his mom's store.*

But the magical super burp really wanted to come out and play.

Cling-clang. Fling-flang. The bubbles were **beating on his bladder** and leaping over his lungs.

Boing-bong. The bubbles trampled onto George's tongue.

Gling-glong. They gathered on his gums.

And then . . .

B-U-U-U-R-P!

Bubble, bubble, George was in trouble.

"Dude! No!" Alex shouted.

Dude, yes! The magical super burp was free. Now George had to do whatever the burp wanted to do.

And what the burp wanted to do was have a **snowball fight**!

George's hands reached down for some snow. They packed it into a tight ball and . . .

Bam! George **pelted** Alex right in the leg with the snowball.

"Hey!" Alex shouted. "Okay. You asked for it!" He bent down to pick up some snow of his own.

Bam! Bam! Bam! Bam! Before Alex
could even stand up, George pelted him
with four more snowballs—right in the
rear end.

Normally, George would never have
been able to make that many snowballs
that fast. But it's a little-known fact
that magical super burps are **snowball-
making** *machines*.

Alex stood up. He tried to run away
from the oncoming snowballs.

But the burp was ready for him.

George threw a snowball at Alex's head with his left hand. He threw a snowball at Alex's **belly** with his right hand.

Alex tried to leap out of the way.

George threw a snowball at Alex's knees. He threw another at his shoulder.

Alex moved to the left.

Bam! George got him in the **gut**.

Alex jumped to right.

Bam! George slammed him in the ribs.

"George, stop that right now!"

George heard a **familiar voice**. He turned around to see his mother. She had come outside to see what was going on.

"Get back to work!" his mother told him. "I need this sidewalk shoveled so my customers can get through."

George wanted to get back to work. He really did. But burps don't like to work. Burps just want to **have fun**.

So George made another snowball. And another. And another. Then he started *juggling* the snowballs. Throwing and catching. Throwing and catching.

George's mom walked toward him, scolding, "Stop that now. I'm not asking you. I'm telling you!"

"Dude! Stop!" Alex pleaded

But George *couldn't* stop. The burp wouldn't let him. *Throw. Catch. Throw . . .*

SPLAT! A snowball hit George's mom, right **on top of her head**.

Her eyes grew really big. She was really surprised.

Pop! Just then, George felt something **burst** in the bottom of his belly. All the air rushed out of him. The magical super burp was gone.

But George was still there. And so was his mom. She had snow in her hair.

It was **dripping down her cheeks** and
over her nose.

Alex didn't look any happier. He was
staring at all the snow he was going to

have to shovel **all over again** now that George had thrown it all over the place.

"What do you have to say for yourself?" George's mother asked him angrily.

George **opened his mouth** to say, "I'm sorry." And that's exactly what came out.

"Not as sorry as you're going to be if you don't start shoveling," his mother said.

George picked up his shovel and got right back to work.

He frowned as his mom walked back into her craft shop. Stupid super burp. It was always getting him in trouble. And it never stuck around long enough to take the blame.

Chapter 2

"Can you believe **how much money** we earned yesterday?" George asked Alex as the boys walked home with Chris after school the next day.

"I made a list of all the things I want to buy," Alex said. "It was two pages long."

"Too bad you were busy," George told Chris. "You could have been **rich**, too."

Chris shrugged. "I got a lot of drawing done," he said. "I think this may be the best Toiletman comic I've ever done."

Just then, Julianna came running to catch up with the boys. "I'm sorry my dad **wouldn't hire you**," she said. "He always makes me and my sister do the shoveling."

"It's okay," George said. "Pretty much everyone else in town hired us."

"Yeah, we're rich," Alex added happily.

"Ha-ha-ha-ha!" Louie Farley interrupted. "You guys? *Rich?*"

"We made a lot of money yesterday," Alex insisted. "More than you did."

"That's the point," Louie said. "When you're rich, you pay *other* people to do your work. That's why my dad paid *you* to shovel our walk while I stayed inside."

"He's right," said Louie's friend Max.

"Louie's *always* right," Louie's other pal Mike added.

George hated when Louie **bragged** about how rich his family was. So he basically hated Louie all the time, because that's all Louie ever talked about. There was nothing worse than hearing Louie talk about money.

"Georgie!"

Okay, maybe hearing Sage call him *Georgie* was worse.

George turned around. Sure enough, there was Sage. She was doing the **weird eyelash-batting thing** she did whenever she saw George.

So George did that eyeball-rolling thing *he* did every time Sage called him Georgie. "What do you want?" he asked her.

"I want to predict our future," Sage replied. "With a **real fortune-teller**."

Gulp. "What do you mean *our* future?" George asked her.

Sage pulled a piece of **folded paper** out of her jacket pocket. "My cousin made this fortune-teller for me," she told the other kids. "She said it **never lies**."

"You're going to tell the future with some **wrinkled-up paper**?" George asked.

Sage stuck her fingers into the pockets she had folded into the paper. "First I tell the fortune-teller my favorite color. *B-L-U-E*." Sage opened and closed the paper fortune-teller four times as she spelled the word. "Now I pick my favorite place. *B-E-A-C-H*." She opened and closed the paper fortune-teller five times as she spelled.

"What does that have to do with the future?" Julianna asked her.

"Watch," Sage replied. "Now I count out my favorite number. And then, when I stop, I lift up the flap. That will give me the first initial of **my special guy**."

George groaned.

"My favorite number is five," Sage continued. She opened and closed the paper fortune-teller. "One . . . two . . . three . . ."

George really hoped that thing didn't open up on the letter *G*.

"Five," Sage finished. She **smiled** at George. "Are you ready to hear our future?" She began to open the flap. "My special guy's name begins with . . . *what?*"

"What's it say?" George asked her.

"*M.*" **Sage shook her head.** "That can't be right."

"*M,*" Julianna thought out loud. "That could be Max. Or Mike."

Max and Mike stared at each other nervously.

George didn't care which one of them it was. He was just glad it wasn't him.

"Do you want to stop for **a snack**?" Alex asked Chris and George a few minutes later as they turned the corner onto Main Street.

"I don't have any money for a snack," Chris replied. "I spent every penny I had on **new drawing supplies**. But my mom baked cookies yesterday. So if you want—"

Before Chris could finish his sentence, Max and Mike came running from behind. They **raced around** George and his friends, and zoomed down the block.

"Hey, Louie, wait for me!" Max cried out.

"And me," Mike added.

"Those guys can't be without Louie

for a second," Alex said.

"But I never saw them run *that* fast to catch up to him before," Chris added.

Just then, Sage's voice rang out. "Maxie! Mikey! Where are you going?"

George laughed. That explained why Louie's pals were **running so fast**. They weren't running *to* Louie. They were running away *from* Sage.

"Look at them go!" George laughed. "They're practically flying."

"WHOA!"

"WHOOPS!"

George watched as Max and Mike *really* flew—right into the air after **slipping on the ice**—and crashed right into Louie, knocking him into a snow pile.

"What the . . . ?" Louie shouted, as he fell face-first into the snow.

George laughed so hard he **snorted**. "This is better than TV," he said.

"No kidding," Chris agreed.

Alex turned around. "It's about to get even better," he said.

George turned around just in time to see Sage running in his direction. "Oh brother," he **groaned**.

But this time, Sage ran right past George and over to Max and Mike.

"There you are, Maxie and Mikey," she said. "Thanks for waiting for me."

"We weren't waiting," Mike said.

"No way," Max added.

Sage pretended she **didn't hear** that. "Where are we going for snacks?" she asked.

"I'm going for pizza," Louie replied, pointing at Mr. Tarantella's Pizza Palace.

"I'm having pizza, too, then," Max said. "I always have my after-school snack with Louie."

"Well, so do *I*," Mike insisted.

"**Pizza** it is," Sage said. "Let's go, guys."

George grinned. It was great the way Sage had just **completely ignored** him.

"So do you guys want to come over for those cookies?" Chris asked Alex and

George. "They're the really good kind. **With sprinkles.**"

George shook his head. "I want to watch Mike and Max deal with Sage. It's going to be **hilarious**."

"Pizza it is then!" Alex agreed.

"I can't," Chris said, shaking his head. "I told you, I'm out of money."

"Oh right," George said. "Well, **don't worry** about *that*."

Chris started to smile.

"We'll call you after and tell you what happens with Sage, Max, and Mike," George continued. "I promise."

Chris stopped smiling.

"Yeah, Chris," Alex added. "We'll give you **every detail**."

"Oh. Okay." Chris looked down and kicked sadly at the ground. "I guess I'll **see you guys later**, then," he muttered quietly.

Then he began walking home, all by himself.

George turned to Alex. "Come on," he said. "**We gotta hurry.** I don't wanna miss a minute of this."

Chapter 3

"I want to sit next to Louie," Max said.

"No way," Mike said. "You sat next to him last time."

"We can *both* sit next to him," Max suggested. He slid into **the booth** and sat on Louie's left.

"Good idea." Mike slid into the booth on Louie's right.

George looked over at their table and laughed. Louie looked like the **baloney** in the middle of a Max-and-Mike sandwich.

Sage sat down across the table and smiled brightly. "Now I can look at both my special guys at the same time," she told Max and Mike.

Max and Mike both groaned.

George started laughing. "This is awesome," he said. "I can't believe Chris is **missing it**."

Just then, Mr. Tarantella walked over to Alex and George's table.

"Hi, Alex," the pizzeria owner said with a big grin. "What will you have?"

"I'd like a **pepperoni slice** and an orange soda," Alex told him.

"Sure thing." Mr. Tarantella turned to George and frowned. "What do *you* want?"

"I'd like a slice with pepperoni. *Please*," George added, trying to be extra polite.

Mr. Tarantella wrote down the order and nodded. Then he walked away.

"Ever since the burp made me go all **wacko** here, Mr. Tarantella has hated me," George whispered to Alex. "Half the shop owners in town hate me."

Alex was the only person George could talk to about the burp. George hadn't told him about his **terrible secret**. Alex was just so smart, he had figured it out. And not only had he promised to keep it a secret, he'd promised to try to help George find a cure!

"That burp is trouble," Alex agreed. "But I think I might have actually found **a cure**."

George wanted to believe him. But he'd tried lots of Alex's burping cures—everything from drinking an **onion milkshake** to pouring gallons of ice-cold water down his throat—and he was still burping.

"I don't have to drink spicy mustard, do I?" George asked. "Because that nearly **burned my tonsils out**."

Alex shook his head. "You just have to let me **hold your hand**."

George gave him a strange look. "I have to *what*?"

"It's called acupressure," Alex explained. "If you put pressure on a certain part of your hand, it gets rid of **the gas** in your stomach. And since gas causes burps—"

"But the burp starts in my stomach and comes out my mouth," George interrupted. "My hand has nothing to do with it."

"I know," Alex agreed. "But there's something called *chi energy* that floats through **your whole body**. If your chi gets blocked somewhere, you can start to feel lousy. Or in your case, gassy."

"And this acupressure thing will unblock my chi?" George asked.

Alex nodded. "Yup. And once your chi is free, the bubbles will just disappear."

George gave him a **funny look**. "This sounds really weird."

"Acupressure has been around for centuries," Alex assured him.

"I guess it's **worth a try**," George said with a shrug.

Alex began pressing George's hand. "I'll start here between your thumb and your pointer finger—" Alex began.

"I call losers!" Louie's voice rang out from across the pizzeria. "And by losers, I mean George!"

Quickly, George **yanked** his hand away. "What are you talking about?" he asked Louie nervously.

"I want to thumb-wrestle you next," Louie replied.

"We're not thumb-wrestling," Alex began. "We're . . . *ouch!*" Alex stopped talking as George **kicked him** under the table. "Why did you do that?" he asked.

George shook his head. He didn't want Alex blurting out anything about the burp or how they were looking for a cure.

Alex got the message. So he grabbed George's hand again and **pretended** to thumb-wrestle. Quickly, he pushed George's thumb down into his palm.

"It's your turn, Louie," Alex said.

Louie stood up and **cracked his knuckles**, loudly.

"Maybe we should bet on it," he said.

"Loser buys the winner's slice."

George had done a lot of shoveling for his money. He wasn't sure he wanted to chance losing any of it to Louie. Still, if he didn't take the bet, it would seem like **he was chicken**. And he couldn't let Louie think that.

"It's a bet," he said finally.

"Good." Louie smiled. "I like my pizza with **extra anchovies**."

George looked at Louie's thumb. The nail was all chewed, and there were little **scaly red patches** around the nail where Louie had bitten off the skin. Yuck!

"What are you waiting for?" Louie asked him.

"Nothing," George said. By now Max, Mike, and Sage had **gathered around** the booth. Alex was staring, too. There was no getting out of it. He grabbed Louie's hand.

"One, two, three, four," Alex said loudly. **"I declare a thumb war!"**

George pushed hard, trying to get Louie's thumb to go down.

Louie pushed hard, trying to get George's thumb to go down.

Then . . . *uh-oh!* George felt something awful—even worse than Louie's **chewed-up thumb**. The magical super burp was back—and it wanted in on the action.

George couldn't let the burp out. Not here. Not now. If the burp caused any **more trouble**, Mr. Tarantella would surely ban George from the Pizza Palace for life.

George knew he should get out of there

as fast as he could. But that would mean **forfeiting to Louie**.

There was only one thing to do. George was going to have to squelch that belch—without letting go of Louie's thumb! *But how?*

George was going to have to spin those bubbles back down to his toes, like **water swirling down a drain**. It had worked before! Hopefully it would work now.

George leaped to his feet, pulling Louie with him.

"Hey!" Louie shouted as he got yanked up. "No fair."

George started turning around and around **in a circle**.

So Louie started turning around and around in a circle. "Go, Louie, go!" Max cheered.

"Louie, Louie, he's our man," Mike shouted. "If he can't beat him, no one can!"

George barely heard Max and Mike **cheering**. He was too busy spinning around.

Spin, spin, spin. Then suddenly . . . *the bubbles started to sink back down toward George's toes*! It was working!

So George **kept spinning**. Around and around he went.

So around and around Louie went.

The bubbles knocked at George's knees and clipped at his calves.

George kept turning.

So Louie kept turning.

The bubbles **tickled George's toes** and . . .

Pop! George felt something burst in his belly. All the air rushed out of him. The magical super burp was gone

Quickly, George **plopped down** in his seat.

So Louie plopped down in his seat.

George pushed at Louie's thumb.
Louie pushed at George's thumb.
And then . . .
SLAM! George forced Louie's thumb
all the way down!

"George is the winner!" Alex shouted excitedly.

George smiled. Alex sure had that one wrong. George wasn't **just a winner**. He was a DOUBLE winner. Not only had he beaten Louie, he'd also squelched the belch.

"No way did George win," Louie said. "You're **not allowed** to stand up and spin around when you thumb-wrestle."

"Then why did *you* stand up and spin around?" Alex asked him.

"Because I wasn't gonna let go and . . ." Louie put his head in his hands. **"I feel dizzy,"** he said.

George smiled. "And I feel *hungry*," he said. Just then, Mr. Tarantella brought over **their slices**.

George smiled up at the pizza-shop owner. "Thanks," he said happily. "Put mine on Louie's tab. He's paying today."

Chapter 4

"I'm telling you, Chris, it was amazing," George said as the boys sat down for lunch in the school cafeteria. "Louie was **so mad** that I beat him."

"It was pretty unbelievable," Alex said. "I've never seen a thumb-wrestling match **like that one** ever—until yesterday."

"I *still* haven't seen one like that," Chris said sadly. "Because I wasn't there."

"Maybe next time," Alex told him.

"Oh no," George insisted. "There's not going to be a next time. I'm never touching Louie's **disgusting** chewed-up thumb again."

Just then, Julianna sat down at the table. She smiled at Chris. "Thanks for the Evite to the local artists' **comic book party**," she told him. "I can't wait to come."

"Oh yeah, the party," George said to Chris. "I got my Evite last night, too. I almost forgot about your comic being published next week. I'll be there, too."

Chris frowned. "You almost forgot about the **most important thing** in my whole life?" he asked George.

George shrugged. "I guess I was just so excited about this thumb-wrestling match and all."

Chris didn't say anything. He pulled out his sketchpad and colored pencils and began to draw.

"It's **really cool** that Rodney is throwing that party," Alex said. "He must think this Toiletman comic book is going to be amazing. You can count me in for sure."

"Well, it's not just a party for me," Chris said **without looking up** from his drawing. "There are three other local artists who will have comic books being sold at the store at the same time. But it is really cool that he's throwing us a party."

Just then, Max and Mike came running into the cafeteria.

"Why are they in such a hurry?" Julianna asked. "**Tuna hoagies** aren't *that* great."

A moment later, Sage came racing through the cafeteria doors. "Wait for me, Mikey," she called out. "You too, Maxie."

George laughed. "That's why," he said.

"Sage is **really obsessed** with those guys," Alex said with a laugh. "I can't believe she really thinks a piece of paper can predict **the future**."

"I wish I could predict *my* future," Chris said. "I wonder if my comic book will do well. **I really hope so.**"

"How many people did you invite to the party?" Julianna asked him.

"A lot," Chris said. "The whole fourth

grade. And my family. And a couple of kids from my **art class**. You guys can all bring extra people if you want, too. The more people, the better."

"If everyone you invited buys one of your comic books, it will be **a best seller**," George said. "You'll be rich."

Louie plopped his tray down on the table across the table from George and **snickered**.

"Rich? From a *comic book*?" Louie said. He shook his head. "You guys **crack me up**."

"It's not about making money," Chris explained. "I just really want everyone to like what I've been working so hard on."

"You're an idiot," Louie told him. "*Everything* is about making money. Or at least it should be."

"My sister says we should each buy a copy," Julianna said. "She thinks they could be collector's items. Will you **autograph** them for us?" she asked Chris.

Chris nodded. "Sure, if you want me to," he said.

"You want *his* autograph?" Louie asked, shaking his head. "Why?"

"He might be a **famous comic-book artist** one day," Julianna explained.

"What about me?" Louie said. "I'm a star already."

"What are you talking about?" George asked him.

"I have my own webcast—*Life with Louie*," Louie insisted. "And I'm a Farley. My autograph will be **worth way more** than Chris's someday."

George shook his head. There wasn't a kid in the whole grade who would want Louie Farley's autograph. Well, except Max and Mike.

"I can't believe you guys are **wasting** all this time talking about those comic books," Louie said.

"What would *you* rather talk about, Louie?" George asked. "How about **how you lost** a thumb-wrestling match yesterday? Because I'm still kind of full from that slice of pizza you bought me afterward."

Louie's eyes got small and angry.

"I just don't see what the **big deal** is," Louie told Chris. "It's not like you're the only kid in school who can draw. Didn't you guys see my **self-portrait** hanging in the hall outside the art room last week?"

George laughed. He'd seen it, all right. Louie's nose looked like a **warty pickle** in his drawing.

"Making a comic book isn't just about

drawing," Chris said. "It's about writing, too. A comic book has to **tell a story**. It has to have good characters. And it—"

Suddenly, Louie reached across the table and **yanked** the sketchpad from Chris's hands.

"How about a **sneak peek** at this great story?" he demanded.

"Give that back," Chris said. "It's not finished. It's just a rough sketch."

But Louie didn't hand the sketchpad back. Instead, he looked down at the page Chris had been working on.

"Oh wow," Louie said. A **giant smile** flashed across his face. "This is awesome."

"Way to go, Chris," George said. "You just got a compliment from Louie. He never compliments *anyone*."

"You definitely drew **these two jerks** perfectly," Louie continued. He pointed to George and Alex.

"What?" Alex asked.

"We're in the comic book?" George added. "Wow!"

Chris shrugged. "It's nòt a final draft. I was just **playing around** with an idea."

"Let me see!" George exclaimed, leaping up from his seat to look over Louie's shoulder. "This is so cool. I've never been . . . **Hey, wait a minute.**"

"I told you, it's a rough draft," Chris

explained. "In the ending, I'm gonna—"

"GASSY GEORGE?" George shouted, cutting Chris off mid-sentence. "You called me GASSY GEORGE?"

"Look at the size of that **rear end**," Louie pointed out as he looked at Chris's artwork. He read the caption under the picture. "Gassy George's **giant butt** propels him through space at the speed of *gas*."

George turned **beet red**. He stared at Chris.

Alex laughed. "That is kind of funny, George," he said.

"Oh yeah?" George asked him. "Well, come take a look at the evil Dr. Alex. He's nothing but **a giant head and some feet**. And he has your hair."

"A giant head to hold his humungous *evil* brain," Louie read out loud.

"Evil?" Alex asked Chris. "You think **I'm evil**?"

"No," Chris said. "It's not really you. It's a character. And—"

"But his name is Alex, right?" Alex demanded.

"Well, yeah," Chris said. "But it's not done yet. And—"

"Hey, at least you're smart," George told Alex. **"I'm just gassy."**

Julianna started laughing.

George shot her a look.

"I'm sorry," she apologized. "It was funny. I couldn't help it."

George shook his head. It was bad enough when Louie laughed at him. But now Chris had his other friends **laughing at him**, too.

George looked over at Alex. "Are you finished eating?" he asked him.

"Yeah." Alex glanced at Chris. "I just **lost my appetite**."

"Great," George said. "How about we go build a snowman in the yard this recess—*just the two of us*."

Chris grabbed his sketchpad back from Louie. He looked at George and Alex. "You guys, it's just a rough draft," he insisted. "I haven't actually finished anything yet, and . . ."

George didn't hear the rest of what Chris was saying. He was already halfway across the cafeteria.

But George could hear *Louie*. That creep could be plenty loud when he wanted to be.

"Hey, George!" Louie shouted. "Better turn sideways going outside. It's the only way your ginormous gassy butt will ever fit through the door."

Everyone in the cafeteria stared in George's direction. The kids all started to laugh, although they had no idea what Louie was talking about. Even the cafeteria lady was chuckling.

George was really mad. His friendship with Chris had just gone right down the drain. And it would take a lot more than a superhero with a plunger to save it.

Chapter 5

"I can't believe that jerk Chris **thinks I'm evil**," Alex said as he and George walked home after school that afternoon.

"I can't believe we're calling *Chris* a jerk," George said. "He was the **first friend** I made when I moved here. I never thought he could do something like this."

"I know what you mean," Alex agreed. "Chris was always a **really nice guy**."

"*Was* he?" George asked.

"What do you mean?" Alex asked him.

"Maybe it was all an act," George said slowly. "Maybe Chris was hiding his **true identity**—kind of like a comic book superhero who seems like a regular guy until he puts his cape on."

"You don't really believe Chris has been **putting on an act** all this time, do you?" Alex asked.

"I don't know what to believe," George said. "I'm just glad he thinks I only have a problem with *regular* gas. Can you imagine if he knew about the **magical super burp**? He'd put that in his comic book for sure. Then everyone would know."

"It's definitely a good thing we kept it a secret," Alex said.

"Yeah," George agreed. "We're sort of like a club. **The Secret Keepers Club.**"

Alex smiled. "Exactly," he said. He held up his hand. "I swear that I will never tell your secrets. And I will never be a jerk."

George **raised his hand** in the air. "Same here," he said. Then he got real quiet.

Alex wasn't saying much, either. George figured Alex was feeling the same way he was. They were both really, *really* mad at Chris. But it still seemed **kind of strange** walking home without him.

"You know what we need?" Alex asked George.

"A new friend?" George suggested.

Alex shook his head. "No. What we need is a **clubhouse**."

"Yeah!" George smiled. "That's a great idea. Every club needs a clubhouse. Where should ours be?"

"Well, you have that shed in **your backyard**," Alex suggested. "That would make a good clubhouse."

"No way," George said. "My mom hasn't let me in the shed since I tried **raising hamsters** in there. She's still mad that one of them ate through her sweater."

"Yeah, that was pretty bad," Alex

agreed. He thought for a minute. "How about we *build* a clubhouse? We could make it somewhere else in your backyard."

"We don't have **any wood** or anything," George said. "The only thing in my backyard right now is snow."

"We could build a clubhouse out of snow," Alex suggested. "Kind of like an **igloo**. Then when the snow melts, we could get some wood and build a real clubhouse."

"That's a **good idea**," George agreed.

"And we don't even have to make a big clubhouse," Alex continued. "After all, there are only the two of us in the club."

"Yep," George agreed. "And that's just how it's **gonna stay**!"

"Well, this isn't exactly a clubhouse," George said an hour later as he looked at the lumps of snow he and Alex had **shoved together** in his backyard.

"It's more like a snow *fort*," Alex said. "Kind of."

George shook his head. "It doesn't look like any snow fort I've ever seen."

"Chris would have been able to build a real clubhouse out of snow," Alex admitted. "And he probably would have made a few **ice sculptures** to decorate it."

George knew that was true. Chris made great ice sculptures. He was an **amazing artist**.

An amazing artist who draws bad guys with giant gassy butts and huge heads.

"We don't need Chris," George told Alex. "We can make this better **all by ourselves**."

He picked up a big pile of snow and started forming it into the shape of a brick.

Alex frowned. "Can we work on it later?" he asked. "My hands are **freezing**."

George's hands were ice cold, too. So were his feet. And his nose. Even his *tonsils* felt cold.

"Let's go inside and have some of my dad's famous double-chocolate **hot cocoa**," George suggested. "He just bought a huge bag of mini marshmallows."

"Yum!" Alex exclaimed. "Maybe while we're inside we can come up with a **secret club handshake**."

"Sure," George agreed. He tried **wiggling** his fingers inside his cold, wet gloves. "As soon as I can move my hands again."

"So, what kinds of things should we do in our club?" Alex asked George a few minutes later as the boys sat in George's kitchen.

George took a sip of his hot chocolate. "I know one thing we're *not* doing," he said. "We're not going to that **stupid party** Rodney is throwing for Chris this Saturday."

"Agreed," Alex said. "We're boycotting!"

George gave him a funny look. "What does **being a boy** have to do with anything?" he asked. "And why would you need a cot? You have a bed."

Alex laughed. "No," he said. "*Boycotting.* It means we're not going because we're protesting what Chris did."

Oh. That made more sense.

"You want to stand outside the store and **protest**?" George asked. "Like with signs and everything?"

Alex shook his head. "I'm mad, but that would be *too* mean," he said. "Like something an **evil genius** might do."

"And you don't want to be anything like that Dr. Alex character in the Toiletman comic," George agreed.

"Just like you don't want to be **gassy** all the time," Alex added.

"You can say that again," George said. He thought for a minute. "I have an idea. Instead of going to the party, we could go see the scary-movie marathon at Beaver Brook Movie Theater. I saw the poster last week. They're showing five **freaky flicks** all in a row."

"I can afford to go to the movies this weekend," Alex said. "I still have plenty of money left from when we were shoveling."

"Me too," George said. "And since Louie paid for my pizza the other day, I even have enough for **soda and popcorn**."

"Perfect!" Alex said. "We're gonna have more fun than we would have had at that party."

"*Much* more," George agreed. He tried to sound like he meant it. But part of him **wasn't so sure**.

Chapter 6

"So how was work?" Alex asked George as the boys left Mr. Furstman's Pet Shop together on Saturday afternoon.

George worked at the **pet shop** every Saturday. Mr. Furstman was probably the only store owner left in Beaver Brook who was **happy** to see George when he walked into his shop. (Except George's mom, of course.) Sure, the magical super burp had shown up at the pet shop once or twice. But Mr. Furstman had never **gotten angry** with all the trouble the burp caused. He actually thought George was funny.

"Same old stuff. Stopped a fight between two hamsters. Fed crickets to the lizards. Cleaned **poop** out of the parakeet cage." George smiled at Alex's grossed-out expression. "It's a tough job, but somebody has to do it. And besides, now I have enough money to get chocolate-covered raisins with my popcorn."

"Excellent," Alex said. "I read the schedule this morning. The first **scary movie** is a really old one called *Tentacles of Terror*."

"I love that movie," George said. "There's this giant octopus that comes out of Lake Michigan and squirts **black gunk** all over Chicago."

"I've seen it before, too," Alex said. "The octopus has got eight really strong green arms. He yanks a giant skyscraper out of the ground with **just one tentacle**."

George laughed. "Yeah I remember

seeing it on TV one night while I was having a **sleepover** at Chr—" George stopped himself. "I mean, at *you-know-who*'s house."

"Yeah, *you know who* is lucky to have a TV in his room," Alex said. "Sleepovers are—I mean *were*—always great at his house."

George frowned. "It'll be better to see those **giant tentacles** on a big movie screen, anyway," he said, forcing a smile.

"Definitely," Alex agreed.

"Everybody loves scary movies," George said. "We **better hurry** if we want to get good seats. I bet half the school is going to be there."

"Where is everybody?" George asked Alex a few minutes later as they stood in the lobby of the movie theater.

The place was *almost empty*, except for a couple teenagers who were buying popcorn.

"There's no one here from our grade, that's for sure," Alex said.

"You think everyone went to **the party** for Chr—I mean, for *you know who?*" George wondered aloud.

"Could be," Alex said. "But they could have gone for one of the other artists, and not for *you know who.*"

"I thought **at least Louie** would be here," George said, looking around the lobby. Then he stopped himself. "I can't believe I just said that."

"Yeah, things are **really bad** when you're actually *looking* for Louie to show up," Alex added sadly.

"It doesn't matter what anyone else is doing today. We're here. *And we're going to have a great time*," George insisted.

"Exactly," Alex agreed.

"You want to get some **popcorn**?" George asked Alex.

"Good idea," Alex told him.

The boys got in line behind a group of teenage guys.

"I'm going to buy the **super-ginormous** bag of popcorn," Alex said. "It's got to last through five super-scary

movies. Or I could get a box of **gummy worms** and a small popcorn. Or . . ."

George didn't hear the rest of what Alex said. He wasn't paying attention. He couldn't. Because at that very moment, there was something **super-scary** going on. And it wasn't inside the movie theater.

It was inside *George*.

Blink-blunk. Slink-slunk. There were bubbles in his belly. Hundreds of them!

George was starring in his own movie—*The Battle of the Burp.* And it was **a battle** George was losing.

Jing-jang. Cling-clang. The bubbles were wiggling around his waist and ricocheting from his rib cage.

George wanted to ask Alex for help, but he **didn't dare** open his mouth. The burp might slip out if he did.

George had no idea what the burp would do if it **burst out** right here in the middle of the movie theater. All he knew was it would be *ba-a-ad!*

George tried to get Alex's attention. He rubbed his head and patted his belly at the same time. That was the **secret signal** Alex had come up with to let him know there was a burp coming.

But Alex wasn't looking at George. He was **too busy** studying the candy boxes behind the counter.

Some of the teenagers in line were looking at George, though. And they were laughing.

"Neat trick, kid," one of them said.

"It's harder than it looks," another teen said as he tried patting his head and rubbing his belly.

George couldn't believe it. Alex was the only one in the whole line who **didn't see** what he was doing

Flonk-flink. Glonk-glink. Now the bubbles were parachuting from his palate and licking at his—

Uh-oh!

"Nice burp, kid," one of the teenagers said.

But George knew there was **nothing nice** about *this* burp. It was already making George do some really *rotten* stuff. Like climb right over the candy case in the middle of the lobby of the movie theater.

"Get down from there!" the person behind the counter **shouted** at him. "Customers aren't allowed back here."

But the burp wasn't a customer. It was a burp. And burps go wherever they please.

"Dude, no!" Alex tried to grab George's shirt and **pull him** back over to the customer side of the counter. But Alex was no match for the super burp.

George's hands grabbed a box of **red-hot** cinnamon candies from behind

the counter. They ripped open the box, tossing the candies in the air.

George opened his mouth wide and started to **catch the candies** as they fell.

Plop. Plop. Plop.

The teenagers all started **cheering**. "Go, kid! Go, kid! Go, kid!"

George caught some more red-hot candies in his mouth.

Plop. Plop. Plop.

"Owwwww!" George shouted. Those candies were really, REALLY hot!

The next thing George knew, he was racing over to the soda fountain. He **stuck his head** under the orange-soda faucet and opened his lips. Then he pulled on the lever. Orange soda gushed into his mouth. *Aaaaahhhhh!*

The manager of the theater rushed out of his office, shouting, "What do you

think you are doing?" He started racing toward the candy counter. "Catch that kid!" the manager yelled to the girl selling candy.

The candy seller started to chase George. She was **pretty fast**.

But the burp was faster. It made George run away from the candy seller.

The manager circled around the other side of the counter. He **blocked** George from leaving. George turned and tried to run the other way. But the candy seller blocked his path. **George was trapped**.

Burps don't like to be trapped.

So the burp made George do the only thing it could.

"COWABUNGA!" George shouted as he **dove headfirst** into the giant popcorn machine!

Pop! Pop! Pop! Kernels of yellow corn popped all around George's head.

Pop! Pop! Pop!

Pop!

That last pop wasn't a kernel of corn. It was something bursting inside George's belly. It felt like someone had **stuck a pin in a balloon** down there. All the air rushed right out of him.

The magical super burp was gone.

But George was still there. With his **head in the popcorn machine**, and his feet sticking up in the air.

Ugh.

George wasn't going to be seeing any movies today. That was for sure. The stupid super burp had **ruined** things for him, again.

Chapter 7

"Well, at least you **only had to pay** for the candies, and not the soda or the popcorn," Alex said. "That's something."

"We paid for the tickets, too." George frowned and pulled a piece of popcorn **out of his hair**. "And we didn't get to see even one of the movies," he groaned. "This burp is really a pain."

"I'll find you a cure, I promise," Alex told him. "It's just taking longer than I thought. None of the **usual burp cures** seem to work."

"This is no usual burp," George said sadly.

"So what do you want to do now?" Alex asked him.

"We can go to **my house** and watch a movie there," George suggested.

"Sure," Alex agreed. "Why not?"

The boys walked a few more blocks. Suddenly, they heard **music and laughing** coming from the comic-book shop down the street.

"That must be the party," George said.

"Sounds like everyone is having **a lot of fun**," Alex said.

George thought about that. "Yeah," he said. "I guess a lot of people showed up to celebrate Chris's comic being published. He probably doesn't even miss us."

"I kind of **miss him**, though," Alex admitted.

George gave him a look. "You do?" he asked.

"Yeah," Alex said. "Don't you?"

George nodded. "I didn't want to say anything because I thought you were **still mad at him**."

"Nah." Alex shook his head. "I mean, those drawings were kind of mean. But they were funny, too."

"*Gassy* isn't the most horrible thing anyone's ever said about me," George admitted. "Louie's called me **a lot worse**."

"We weren't so nice to Chris, either," Alex pointed out. "We could have gone to his house for cookies after school instead of the pizza place. Or treated him to a slice."

"Yeah," George admitted. "And we did kind of brag **right in front of him** about how much money we earned shoveling."

Alex smiled. "Chris has worked hard on this comic. He's been our friend for a long time—" he began.

"Are you saying you *want* to go to the party?" George asked him.

Alex nodded.

"Me too," George said. "Let's go."

"You made it!" Chris shouted **excitedly** as George and Alex walked into the Made for Mutants Comic Book Shop.

"We couldn't miss this," George told him. **And he meant it.**

Alex looked around the store. "It seems like *all* the kids made it."

"Yeah," Chris said. "And not only that, Rodney told the **newspaper** about it, and they sent a reporter out to interview all the local artists."

"Wow! You're gonna be **famous**, dude," Alex said.

Chris smiled. "I guess."

George pointed to the stack of Toiletman comic books on the counter. "These are the **finished copies**?" he asked.

Chris nodded. "All twenty-two pages." He picked up another copy and turned to the **last page**. "This is how it ends," he said.

George opened to the last page of the comic. His eye went right to the

pictures of Gassy George and Dr. Alex. He
frowned . . .

. . . And then he smiled.

"Check this out," he told Alex. "We
weren't the **bad guys** at all. We were
heroes."

"I told you it wasn't finished yet," Chris said. "Gassy George and Dr. Alex were **double agents**. They were just pretending to be bad to help Toiletman capture—"

"Mean Mr. Moneybags!" Alex and George shouted at the same time as they read from the page.

"He's the real bad guy," Chris said. "He steals from poor people and hides their money in his **tarantula-shaped** safe."

"He looks like Louie," George said.

"Can you think of a better model for a bad guy?" Chris asked.

"Definitely not," George said with a laugh. "So what did Louie say when he saw it?"

"He hasn't," Chris said. "He **won't even look** at any of the comic books. He's just standing there in the corner with Max and Mike."

George glanced over to the corner of the store. Sure enough, Louie was there looking **miserable**—the way Louie *always* looked when he wasn't the center of attention.

Just then, a man walked over to where George, Chris, and Alex were standing. He held up a **pad and pencil** and smiled at Chris.

"So these are the friends you were telling me about," the man said. "The ones who inspired Toiletman's fellow **superheroes**."

"Yep," Chris said. "George and Alex are my best friends." He smiled at his pals. "This is Jimmy Lane. He's a reporter for the *Beaver Brook Gazette*."

"How do you two feel about being used as **characters** in a new comic book?" Jimmy asked.

"Pretty good," George said. And he meant it.

"It's **an honor**," Alex added.

"Especially because the characters help put Mean Mr. Moneybags away," George added.

"Speaking of Mean Mr. Moneybags," Jimmy Lane said to Chris. "Was that character also **inspired** by someone in your life?"

Chris grinned. "Well," he said. "Now
that you mention it . . ."

George **chuckled** to himself. He knew
what was coming. This was about to get
good. *Really* good.

Chapter 8

"WHAT DO YOU MEAN, I'M THE BAD GUY?" Louie shouted from across the room.

Everyone stopped what they were doing and **turned to stare**.

"I didn't say *you* were the bad guy," Jimmy Lane corrected him. "I said that there seems to be some **similarities** between you and the bad guy in Chris's comic book."

Louie glared at Chris. "I'm going to sue you! My dad is a **rich lawyer**. He never loses a case. You're gonna be broke!"

"Yeah, his dad is the best lawyer in the whole world," Max said.

"The whole universe," Mike added.

"He'd lose *this* case," Jimmy Lane told him. "Because Mean Mr. Moneybags isn't really you. He's just a **parody** of a spoiled, rich brat."

"If you sue, you'll be admitting that you're a **spoiled brat**, Louie," George said. "Are you?"

"Go ahead and sue, Louie," Mike added. "You'll win for sure. There's no bigger brat than you."

"Yeah!" Max shouted. "You're the **spoiledest**."

Louie glared at his friends.

Max and Mike shut up really, really fast.

"Yeah . . . well," Louie muttered. "There's **no point** in suing Chris, anyway. He's not going to make any money on this stupid comic book."

Just then, Julianna and her older sister, Sasha, came **running over**. They were each holding a copy of the Toiletman comic book.

"Will you sign this for me?" Sasha asked Chris.

"Sure," Chris said happily. He pulled out a marker and **signed his name**.

"Mine too, please," Julianna said.

Chris signed her comic book, too.

"Oh brother!" Louie groaned. "You two are **ridiculous**. Nobody in his right mind would—"

Before Louie could finish his sentence, a third kid walked over. He was holding **several copies** of Chris's Toiletman comic book.

"Chris, I just bought five of these," he said. "After you sign them, I'm going to keep them in our family safe. When you're famous, I'll sell them for a **fortune**."

Louie's eyes bugged. "Sam?" he said. "You're buying those?"

George started to laugh. Sam was Louie's older brother. Louie thought Sam was the **greatest kid** who ever lived. He was always trying to copy him.

"You should buy some copies of this

comic, too, Louie," Sam said. "Your friend
Chris is really talented. He's going to be a
big deal one day."

"B-b-but . . . ," Louie stammered. He
didn't know what to say to that.

"Georgie!"

Just then, George heard a familiar, **annoying voice** coming from the front of the store. It was Sage. And she was calling him Georgie again.

"There you are," Sage said excitedly as she walked over to where George was standing. She did that crazy **batting-her-eyelashes** thing. "I've been looking for you."

"Um . . . don't you mean you were looking for Max and Mike?" George asked her nervously.

Max and Mike backed as far away from Sage as they could get.

"She said 'Georgie,'" Max told George.

"Yeah, I heard her," Mike agreed.

George had heard her, too. He was just hoping he'd **heard wrong**.

"Oh, I've decided that paper fortune-teller could never be right," Sage told George.

"Why not?" George asked her.

"Well, for one thing, I left it in my pocket when my mom washed my jeans," Sage explained. "It came out of the wash looking like **a blob**. How can a blob of paper predict the future?"

George looked hopelessly at his friends.

"She's got ya there," Alex said with a shrug.

"**Blobby paper** can't predict much," Julianna agreed.

"Blobby Paper . . . ," Chris repeated. "That's a great name for a comic book villain."

Alex and Julianna laughed.

But George didn't think there was **anything funny** about any of this.

"Here's a *real* fortune-teller," Sage said. She pulled out a big purple ball.

"What is that?" George asked her.

"It's a **magic grape ball**," Sage
explained. "It was my mom's when she
was a kid. She said it predicted her life
perfectly. It's much more reliable than a
paper fortune-teller."

Julianna walked over to get a **closer
look** at the plastic grape ball. "How does
it work?" she asked.

"You ask the ball a question. Then you
turn it over, and **your answer appears**.

Watch." Sage looked down at the ball. "Is Georgie the **boy of my dreams?**" she asked.

No. No. No, George thought to himself. *Say no.*

Sage turned the ball over. She looked at **the message** on the bottom and smiled.

"It says, 'Absolutely,'" she said happily. "See, Georgie?" she added, holding the ball out so George could get **a better look**.

Ugh. It said it all right.

But right now, George was only absolutely sure about one thing.

Gurgle-blurgle.

Oh no. Not the magical super burp. Not now. George couldn't turn into **gassy George**—not in front of all these people, and a newspaper reporter!

Schmurgle-durgle.

Hey! Wait a minute. Those weren't bubbles down there. Those were **hunger pains**. *Phew.*

George reached up and pulled a couple of popcorn kernels out of his hair.

Then he popped them into his mouth.
Okay, so **hairy popcorn** wasn't exactly
George's idea of a great snack. But at
least it was something.

Hunger was easy to get rid of. All you
had to do was eat.

Too bad it wasn't **that easy** to get rid
of a magical super burp.

"Georgie," Sage said as she batted her
eyelashes up and down. "Do you want to
go out for **ice cream** after the party? Just
the *two* of us?"

George rolled his eyes. He wouldn't
mind getting rid of Sage, either. She was
as annoying as the super burp . . .

Well, *almost* as annoying, anyway.

About the Author

Nancy Krulik is the author of more than 150 books for children and young adults, including three *New York Times* Best Sellers and the popular Katie Kazoo, Switcheroo books. She lives in New York City with her family, and many of George Brown's escapades are based on things her own kids have done. (No one delivers a good burp quite like Nancy's son, Ian!) Nancy's favorite thing to do is laugh, which comes in pretty handy when you're trying to write funny books! You can follow Nancy on Twitter: @NancyKrulik.

About the Illustrator

Aaron Blecha was raised by a school of giant squid in Wisconsin and now lives with his family by the south English seaside. He works as an artist designing funny characters and illustrating humorous books, including the one you're holding. You can enjoy more of his weird creations at www.monstersquid.com.